Five little men in a flying saucer flew round the world one day.
They looked left and right, but they didn't like the sight . . .

Four little men in a flying saucer flew round the world one day.
They looked left and right, but they didn't like the sight . . .

flying saucer flew round the world one day
and right, but they didn't like the sight . . .

lying saucer flew round the world one day, and right, but he didn't like the sight . . .

...ying saucer flew round the world one day,
left and right, so nobody saw the sight...

... and no one flew away!

... so they decided to stay!

Five little men in a flying saucer flew round the world one day.
They looked left and right, but they didn't like the sight ...

... so one man flew away!

Four little men in a flying saucer flew round the world one day.
They looked left and right, but they didn't like the sight ...

... so one man flew away!

Three little men in a flying saucer flew round the world one day.
They looked left and right, but they didn't like the sight ...

... so one man flew away!

Two little men in a flying saucer flew round the world one day.
They looked left and right, but they didn't like the sight ...

... so one man flew away!

One little man in a flying saucer flew round the world one day.
He looked left and right, but he didn't like the sight ...

... so then he flew away!

No little men in a flying saucer flew round the world one day.
Not one looked left and right, so nobody saw the sight ...

... and no one flew away!

Five little men in a flying saucer came back to the world one day.
They looked left and right, and they really liked the sight ...

... so they decided to stay!

Five Little Men
in a Flying Saucer

illustrated by
Dan Crisp

Child's Play (International) Ltd
Swindon   Auburn ME   Sydney
© 2005 Child's Play (International) Ltd   Printed in China
ISBN 1-904550-30-4
3579108642
www.childs-play.com